W9-BYY-588

This book belongs to:

_____

_____

_____

First published by Walker Books Ltd.,
87 Vauxhall Walk, London SE11 5HJ

Copyright © 2000 by Lucy Cousins
Lucy Cousins font copyright © 2000 by Lucy Cousins

Illustrated in the style of Lucy Cousins by King Rollo Films Ltd.

Maisy audiovisual series produced by King Rollo Films Ltd.
for Universal Pictures International Visual Programming

Maisy™. Maisy is a registered trademark of Walker Books Ltd., London.

First U.S. paperback edition 2000

Library of Congress Cataloging-in-Publication Data

Cousins, Lucy.
Maisy drives the bus / Lucy Cousins. —1st U.S. ed.
p. cm.
Summary: Maisy the mouse picks up an assortment of passengers as she drives her bus.
ISBN 0-7636-1083-6 (hardcover) — ISBN 0-7636-1085-2 (paperback)
[1. Mice—Fiction. 2. Buses—Fiction. 3. Bus drivers—Fiction.] I. Title.
PZ7.C83175Maed 2000
[E]—dc21   99-054075

12 13 14 15 16 SWT 25 24 23 22 21 20 19 18 17

Printed in Dongguan, Guangdong, China

This book was typeset in Lucy Cousins.
The illustrations were done in gouache.

Candlewick Press
99 Dover Street
Somerville, Massachusetts 02144

visit us at www.candlewick.com

Maisy Drives the Bus

Lucy Cousins

CANDLEWICK PRESS

Maisy is driving her bus today.

Who will be waiting at Bus Stop Number 1?

It's Cyril.

Hello, Cyril.

Little Black Cat
is waiting at Bus
Stop Number 2.

Hello,
Little Black Cat.

Brmm, Brmm!

Who will be waiting at Bus Stop Number 3?

It's Tallulah,
standing in the rain.

Hello, Tallulah.

And here's Eddie at Bus Stop Number 4.

Will there be room on the bus?

Hooray! There's room for everyone.

Brmm, Brmm! Where is Maisy going now?

Bus Stop Number 5.

It's time to get off, everyone.

Oops! Wake up,
Little Black Cat.

This is the last stop.

Bye-bye, everyone.
Bye-bye, Maisy.

Brmm, Brmm!

Lucy Cousins is one of today's most acclaimed author-illustrators of children's books. Her unique titles instantly engage babies, toddlers, and preschoolers with their childlike simplicity and bright colors. And the winsome exploits of characters like Maisy reflect the adventures that young children have every day.

Lucy admits that illustration comes more easily to her than writing, which tends to work around the drawings. "I draw by heart," she says. "I think of what children would like by going back to my own childlike instincts." And what instincts! Lucy Cousins now has more than thirteen million books in print, from cloth and picture books to irresistible pull-the-tab and lift-the-flap books.